MW00885261

*This book is dedicated
to people who have the courage
of their convictions.*

A NOTE ABOUT THE ARTWORK: Tifi and her
brothers are Eurasian red squirrels. While Tifi's
story is fantasy, the illustrations accurately reflect the
plant and animal life these kinds of squirrels—found
throughout Europe and Asia—would typically
encounter.

Copyright © 1996 by Nord-Süd Verlag AG, Gossau Zürich, Switzerland
First published in Switzerland under the title *Das Eichhörnchen und der Mond*
English translation copyright © 1996 by North-South Books Inc.

First published in the United States, Great Britain, Canada,
Australia, and New Zealand in 1996 by North-South Books,
an imprint of Nord-Süd Verlag AG, Gossau Zürich, Switzerland.

Distributed in the United States by North-South Books Inc., New York.

Library of Congress Cataloging-in-Publication Data is available.
A CIP catalogue record for this book is available from The British Library.
ISBN 1-55858-530-3 (TRADE BINDING) 10 9 8 7 6 5 4 3 2 1
ISBN 1-55858-531-1 (LIBRARY BINDING) 10 9 8 7 6 5 4 3 2 1
Printed in Belgium

ELEONORE SCHMID

THE SQUIRREL AND THE MOON

TRANSLATED BY ROSEMARY LANNING

NORTH-SOUTH BOOKS

NEW YORK / LONDON

THE FULL MOON shone brightly the night the four baby squirrels were born. Small and hairless, with their eyes still tightly closed, they lay huddled in the round nest their mother had lined with soft hay, moss, and leaves.

The newborn babies spent most of their time sleeping. They changed slowly from pink to rusty red as their fur grew and covered their bodies.

At last their eyes opened. The first things Tifi, the youngest, saw were her mother's beautiful round eyes.

When the wind blew, it gently rocked the squirrels' nest. Tifi liked that. And she loved to lie in the middle of the nest, with her brothers around her. There was something about circles that made her happy: a circle of squirrels in a circular nest, with their mother's round eyes watching over them.

One day mother squirrel told her children they were big enough to explore the world, and the young animals almost tumbled out of their nest in excitement.

Mother squirrel taught her children how to cling to the branches with their sharp claws, and how to use their tails for balancing. Then she plucked a pinecone and showed them how to pull back the scales and nibble the seeds. Tifi squeaked with delight as she watched the empty seed cases spin through the air like tiny propellers.

As the days passed, the young squirrels became stronger and more daring. Soon they were leaping from tree to tree, exploring further and further from the nest.

One hot day when Tifi went looking for something to drink, she found a pond. A startled frog hopped into the still water, sending ripples hurrying to the shore.

"Circles!" cried Tifi, and she dropped some acorns into the pond to set more ripples running across the water. This was such fun that she did it again and again, only stopping when hunger drove her to find food.

The roundest things taste best, Tifi decided as she munched juicy berries and nuts and little round mushrooms. And by evening her stomach was full and round too.

The next morning mother squirrel called Tifi and her brothers together. "Summer will soon be over," she told them. "Go and find as much food as you can, and be sure to store some of it for the long winter."

The young squirrels sprang from tree to tree, and spread out to the four corners of the wood. They found ripe fruit, nuts, and seeds wherever they went, and when they had eaten their fill they hid spare food in hollows or buried it in the ground. Then they covered their stores with earth and twigs, as their mother had taught them.

Tifi ate and stored only round nuts. Beechnuts were too spiky and pointed for her taste.

One evening Tifi saw the full moon rise above the treetops at the other side of the wood. As the sky darkened, the moon rose higher and became even more luminous. Tifi stared and stared at the gleaming circle of light. "So beautiful and so round," she murmured.

From then on Tifi stayed up late every night, waiting for the moon. But every night she had a longer wait. And each night the moon was less round. "What is the matter? Why are you so thin?" Tifi asked the moon. "Are you hungry? Do you like to eat round things too?"

Tifi decided to gather the roundest, tastiest hazelnuts for the moon, and to bury them in a clearing where the moon would easily find them.

But the moon went on waning. Finally it was nothing but a thin crescent, appearing briefly at the end of the night. Tifi slept all day and waited all night to see the moon, but one night it didn't appear at all.

Tifi searched everywhere for the moon. "Did you see where it went?" she asked the other squirrels. But they couldn't help. So she went to the very edge of the forest. There were many lights there, but none were round and white like the moon.

An owl flew down and perched beside her.

"Do you know where the moon went?" Tifi asked.

"No one knows that," the owl replied. "The moon comes and goes and there's nothing to be done about it."

But Tifi couldn't just wait, and trust, and watch the sky, hoping the moon would come back to join the twinkling stars.

"How very hungry it must be," she said, and worked even harder to increase her special store of nuts for the moon. As she worked, she often looked up at the sky. Then one day, between the white clouds, Tifi saw a pale crescent moon. It curved the other way this time. "Is it you?" asked Tifi, puzzled. "Have you turned around?" There was no answer, but night by night the moon grew rounder and stayed longer in the sky, until one night it was a perfect white circle once again. "Aaah," sighed Tifi happily. "I knew it needed food to grow round and fat again."

Tifi had been so busy that she didn't notice the weather growing cold. The leaves were turning brown and falling from the trees.

Tifi hurried back to the old nest. One by one her brothers returned. All had grown fit and strong. "Where have you been? What have you been doing?" they asked her.

"I found the lovely round moon," Tifi told them. "And I buried nuts for it."

Her brothers laughed, but that night they squeezed back into the old nest and said, "Come on, Tifi. Lie in the middle, as you always used to, and tell us about your moon.

The weeks that followed were dark and misty. Rain fell frequently, and the squirrels rarely left their nest. One night winter silently arrived. In the morning the ground was covered in snow. Tifi and her brothers snuggled close, with their bushy tails curled around them like blankets. In this cold weather they slept a lot.

Now and then, when hunger woke them, they crept outside. "Tifi, come and help us look for stores," called her brothers, crawling slowly down the tree trunk, their legs stiff and their paws prickled by ice crystals. They were growing thin, and their stores were getting very low. Often her hungry brothers said to Tifi, "Show us where you buried nuts for the moon." But even though she was hungry too, Tifi always refused. "The moon needs them," she said.

Spring came and the sap rose. Buds swelled and burst into new leaves. There was plenty of food again.

In summer Tifi built a nest and had babies of her own. One night, when the moon was full, Tifi took her children to the clearing. "Come and look!" she cried excitedly. "The moon has given us these tiny trees in return for the nuts. See how they are growing in a circle? Isn't that wonderful!"

In the years that followed, Tifi added to her secret store, even in the hardest winters when food was scarce. And it seemed to her that the moon repaid her, over and over again. For the tiny saplings grew into a great thicket of hazel trees, where she and her children and her children's children played and fed for ever after.

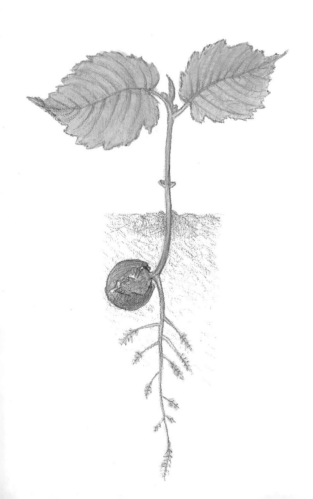